Sejal Sinha
Battles Superstorms

Sejal Sinha

Battles Superstorms

Science is cool!

Maya

BY MAYA PRASAD ⚡ ILLUSTRATED BY ABIRA DAS

ALADDIN
New York London Toronto Sydney New Delhi

ALADDIN

An imprint of Simon & Schuster Children's Publishing Division

1230 Avenue of the Americas, New York, New York 10020

First Aladdin paperback edition May 2023

Text copyright © 2023 by Maya Prasad

Illustrations copyright © 2023 by Abira Das

Also available in an Aladdin hardcover edition.

All rights reserved, including the right of reproduction in whole or in part in any form.

ALADDIN and related logo are registered trademarks of Simon & Schuster, Inc.

For information about special discounts for bulk purchases, please contact Simon & Schuster Special Sales at 1-866-506-1949 or business@simonandschuster.com.

The Simon & Schuster Speakers Bureau can bring authors to your live event. For more information or to book an event contact the Simon & Schuster Speakers Bureau at 1-866-248-3049 or visit our website at www.simonspeakers.com.

Designed by Heather Palisi

The illustrations for this book were rendered digitally.

The text of this book was set in Berling Nova Text Pro.

Manufactured in the United States of America 0323 OFF

2 4 6 8 10 9 7 5 3 1

CIP data for this book is available from the Library of Congress.

ISBN 9781665911788 (hc)

ISBN 9781665911771 (pbk)

ISBN 9781665911795 (ebook)

For Commander B:
you inspire me every day
—M. P.

To Ani:
My light in stormy weather
—A. D.

CONTENTS

Sejal Sinha

Battles Superstorms

CHAPTER ONE
Professor Cheetah and the Moon Mission

Cardboard boxes have a lot of magic that grown-ups just don't get. They can turn into anything and take you anywhere. Need a submarine to go to the bottom of the sea? Need a machine to dig to the center of the earth? Need a train to take you deep into a mine filled with crystals?

A cardboard box can do the job.

"Another successful mission!" I said as we landed back on the shaggy rug in my family's basement.

"Excellent work! I can't wait to examine my moon samples," Professor Cheetah said, giving me a high five.

She was the smartest of all my stuffed animals—and my best stuffie friend. She'd been my copilot on our cardboard box trip to the moon, and now she hopped out of the box and took the samples to her laboratory (also known as the toy shelf).

Just then I heard the doorbell ring upstairs. As she always did, my puppy started barking super ferociously. You couldn't tell she weighed only five pounds, because she sounded way bigger.

"Oof!" said Professor Cheetah. "Does Fluff Monster need to be so loud? I'm trying to concentrate!"

Professor Cheetah took science very seriously. I liked learning how things worked, but mostly went on the missions for the adventure.

Right now, though, I was excited to be back home. Because today was Diwali! My favorite Indian holiday, all about light winning over darkness. We dress up in fancy clothes and make pretty designs with colored sand out on the porch. We light up the house with candles, play with sparklers in the backyard, and eat a huge yummy feast. With plenty of sweets for dessert, too.

Plus, my aunt, uncle, and cousin Mira were coming to celebrate with us. I couldn't wait! Just one problem. I hadn't cleaned up the basement even though Mom had told me to. Oops.

I started picking up the pieces of my little brother Abu's train set since he was "helping" Dad with dinner. Which probably meant making dinosaur sculptures with poori dough. That sounded more fun than cleaning, but when I had complained, Mom had given me that squinty look she got when she was annoyed. The one that meant she might give me some math problems to do. Mom loved assigning extra homework. She thought our teachers didn't give enough.

I hadn't gotten much picked up before the basement door opened. My cousin Mira came down the steps, my cookies-and-cream-colored pup following excitedly behind her.

"Hi, Sejal," Mira said.

"Hi, Mira!" I dropped the train track piece I was holding and ran to give her a hug.

She hugged me back, but then peeked over at my spaceship. "Don't tell me you're still playing with cardboard boxes!"

CHAPTER TWO
Grown-Up Mira

That wasn't what I'd expected her to say—and her words hurt.

"I wasn't *playing* with it," I told her. "I was going on an adventure. To the moon. Come see the samples that Professor Cheetah collected. They're really cool!"

"Uh-huh." She rolled her eyes.

Professor Cheetah had gotten very quiet. She did that around grown-ups—and other people who didn't believe in cardboard box and stuffie magic. But that was strange. Mira loved her uni-corn stuffie, and they'd both gone on plenty of cardboard box adventures with me and Professor Cheetah before.

Maybe Mira was sad that I'd gone without her?

"We could go again if you want to," I offered.

"No thanks," she said. "We're kind of old for playing pretend, aren't we?"

Mira was nine, one year older than me. Lately she'd been acting too grown-up for the stuff we always used to like. Today she even *looked* grown-up. She was wearing a pink satin lehenga with pretty gold and pink flower designs on the skirt and blouse. Her hair was pulled back into a braid with flower clips. She basically looked like a nine-year-old princess. Meanwhile, I was wearing a faded black T-shirt that said "SCIENCE IS COOL!" with a small rip in the armpit. Mom had told me to change into nice clothes too, but I'd forgotten.

"Our missions are not pretend!" I protested.

I couldn't believe my cousin was acting like cardboard box magic didn't exist. Was this some weird thing that happened to you when you turned nine? Because if that was true, I wanted to stay eight years old. I wanted cardboard box magic forever.

"Right." Mira rolled her eyes again. "Anyway, this place is a mess. Do you need my help to clean up?"

"Don't tell me you like *cleaning* now?"

That was way too grown-up for me. Had everything about her changed?

She laughed. "Not really. Your mom asked me to help, though. She said cleaning is part of the Diwali tradition."

"Yeah, the worst part," I said.

She laughed again. "Pretty much."

At least we were laughing together. I felt a little better.

"Okay, okay, we'll clean," I said. "But after that, let's do the rangoli."

Rangoli was what we called the designs we would make on the porch with colored powder. We made them to welcome blessings and good fortune into our home.

"Sure," Mira said. "Remember the design we made last year? It was so pretty! I have some ideas to make it even better this year."

"Cool!" I said.

Mira loved art, and I loved hanging out with my older cousin. Diwali was always a blast, but this time I wanted it to be the best ever. Making beautiful rangoli and lighting sparklers in the driveway and eating lots of yummy Indian food— all of it would show her that we could still have fun together.

Even if she didn't believe in cardboard box magic.

CHAPTER THREE
Barking Away the Hurricane

We were picking up Abu's train set when the lights flickered off and on. The first time it happened, I wasn't too worried. But then it happened again.

"It must be the storm outside," Mira said. "Did you know there was a hurricane warning on the news?"

"Yeah," I said. "But Mom told me that it was hundreds of miles away, so we don't need to worry."

"She probably didn't want to scare you," Mira said. "But hurricanes can actually travel really fast. We've been learning about them at school. They're spinning storms that form in the ocean. They're also called typhoons or tropical cyclones, and they're powered by warm water."

"Wait, why do they have three names?" I asked. "They're really the same?"

"Yep," Mira said. "The name is just different depending on where they're formed. Like which part of the ocean."

"Um. That's weird."

"Yep," Mira said. "I don't know why scientists are so confusing like that."

"Scientists can be pretty silly," I said, laughing.

I thought science was cool, just like it said on my T-shirt. But sometimes Mira and I would joke about scientists because we have A LOT of them in the family. My mom is an astrophysicist (studying stars and planets). My dad works in neuroscience (stuff about brains). Mira's mom is a software engineer (computer stuff), and her dad is a chemist (um, mixing things together in a tube?).

"Anyway," Mira continued, "the thing is— hurricanes are pretty serious. They can destroy whole cities."

I shivered. "Do you think something bad will happen to us?"

"Our parents will keep us safe," Mira said. "Even if we have to leave town."

I didn't like the idea that we would need to leave our house. Or that it could be destroyed. "But what about Diwali?"

Mira shrugged. "If a hurricane is coming, I guess there won't be a Diwali."

"What?" I yelled. "We can't—"

That's when the lights went off again. Only, this time they didn't come back on right away. It wasn't completely dark in the basement, since there were a couple of small windows with a little bit of afternoon light coming in. Even still, it was hard to see in the shadows.

Fluff Monster decided that barking at the

darkness would be really helpful. "Woof! Woof! Woof!"

"You can't scare away a hurricane by barking," Mira said to Fluff Monster.

But Fluff kept barking. When that didn't work, she switched to a low growl, running around in the shadows. I could hear her little paws padding on the carpet and the clinking sound the charm on her collar made.

"Don't move," I warned Mira. "I don't want us to accidentally step on her."

Fluff was a Havanese, which is a type of small dog. And she was only five months old, so she wasn't even her full size. She could get hurt if we accidentally tripped on her.

"No problem," Mira said. "I've got her."

I heard a licking sound, and Mira giggled. I couldn't believe that Fluff Monster went to her instead of me in the dark. Not fair.

"SAY-JULL! MEE-RUH!" Mom called from the top of the basement stairs. "Girls, are you okay?"

"Yeah, we're fine!" Mira said. "Fluff Monster is keeping us company."

"I hope the lights come back on soon." Mom came down with flashlights for both of us. "But until then, be careful when you're walking around."

Mira put the light under her chin and spoke in a spooky ghost voice. "Boooooo! Boooooo!"

Fluff Monster barked away, of course. "Woof! Woof! Woof!"

14

Then she let out a low growl.

Mira giggled. "It's just me, Fluff."

Fluff growled again, and Mira made an even scarier face into her light. "Booooooo!"

CHAPTER FOUR
A Small Chance of Evacuating

I screamed and ran up the stairs, even though I wasn't really scared of ghosts. Hurricanes seemed much scarier, really. But screaming at something silly made me feel better. Mira chased behind me, booing and laughing at the same time.

"Whoa, no running in the dark!" my aunt scolded as we darted into the living room.

"Sorry, Mausi," I said, slowing down.

The room was lit up with tons of candles, and it looked really cozy and nice. It wasn't just because we had lost power either. For Diwali, we always light at least one candle in every room.

My uncle smiled at me. "Hi, Sejal! Happy Diwali!"

He put a stack of boxes down on the coffee table. There was one with sparklers, one with sand for rangoli, one with yummy coconut burfi, and one with sugary laddoo. Dessert was going to be tasty, but I knew we'd have to wait for that.

"Hi, Mausa! Happy Diwali!" I grabbed the box of colored sand. "Can we make the rangoli designs now?"

After all, I couldn't let a hurricane ruin everything.

"I don't know if that's such a good idea," Ravi Mausa said. "Look outside."

I glanced out the window. Heavy wind shook the trees like they were cinnamon sticks in the blender. The rain hammered hard on our roof.

"Woof! Woof! Woof! Woof!" Fluff Monster tried to scare away the hurricane again.

I scratched her behind the ears. "I don't think

that's going to work. But you're a brave puppy for trying."

Just then Abu came running into the room wearing Mom's frilly yellow apron, which was way too big for him.

"We have to evacuate! We have to evacuate! We have to evacuate!" he yelled.

Fluff Monster got even more excited to have someone who also liked making loud noises to

scare away storms. She chased Abu, and they both ran around the coffee table together in circles.

"Woof! Woof! Woof!" Fluff Monster barked.

"We have to evacuate!" Abu yelled again.

Mom put her hands on her hips. "Abu, the news said there's only a small chance we will have to evacuate."

"But what does 'evacuate' mean?" Abu asked.

"If you don't know, why are you screaming

about it?" Mira asked. "Anyway, it means we'd have to pack our things and go stay in a hotel or someone else's house."

Mom nodded. "It's only a small chance, so let's stay calm. We've had hurricane warnings before, remember?"

Remembering that we had gone through hurricane warnings before did help. A little bit.

CHAPTER FIVE
Light over Darkness

But Abu didn't listen to Mom about staying calm, and kept running. He tripped on the end of his too-big apron and fell onto the carpet, almost on top of Fluff Monster. Luckily, she jumped out of the way in time. Then she licked him to show she wasn't mad at him for nearly smooshing her.

Dad poked his head into the room. "Abu, I thought you were helping me with dinner. I need your extra-special stirring skills!"

I rolled my eyes. How much help could a five-year-old be?

But Mom scooted Abu out toward the kitchen. "Yes, why don't you focus on helping Dad? Good thing we have a gas stove so we can still cook!"

"But don't you think I should pack?" Abu said.

"Not yet, dear," Mom replied.

After he was gone, I sat down on the sofa between my uncle and aunt. "Are you sure we can't at least try to do the rangoli?"

Ravi Mausa put his arm around me. "Sorry, beti. It's too rainy and windy."

"But our porch is covered." I gave the grown-ups my best *please-please-please* look.

Ravi Mausa looked at Sheela Mausi. "What do you think?"

Sheela Mausi shrugged. "It might get messy, but we can try if your mom is okay with it."

I gave Mom another *please-please-please* look with big eyes. It worked.

"Well," she said, "I suppose it is an important part of our tradition. We want to welcome good spirits and good fortune for Diwali. But don't be disappointed if it gets too stormy and we have to go inside. And all that wind might mess up our designs."

"I know, I know." I breathed a sigh of relief. We weren't going to skip the rangoli! I was sure everything would be fine.

Sheela Mausi, Mom, Mira, and I went out to the porch while Ravi Mausa went to help Dad and Abu with the cooking. Fluff Monster came with us, doing her business quickly in the grass and then running back to the covered area. She hated getting her fur wet.

The wind made a loud howling noise, and of course Fluff took that personally.

"Woof! Woof! Woof!" she said to the mean old wind.

Mira wrinkled her nose at the weather. The rain was so hard, it was coming down diagonally into part of the porch.

"It's dry over here," Mom said, pointing.

We all got onto our hands and knees with chalk.

Mira told us her idea for the design, lots of colorful flowers connected in a big spiral. She made the outline, and I carefully spread some purple-colored sand inside a flower petal. The wind blew some of it out of the lines, but it didn't look too bad. Mira started to fill in a hot-pink flower.

Another big gust of wind came, blowing the sand all over the porch. And all over her pretty pink lehenga.

"Oh no!" Mira cried. "Now I'm a mess, and the rangoli is completely messed up. This was a terrible idea!"

She ran inside and slammed the door behind her.

Mira had never cared about her clothes so much before. This was new, too. My eyes filled with tears. Diwali was supposed to be about light winning over darkness. But what if the hurricane won instead?

CHAPTER SIX
Mira and the Hot-Pink Smudge

Mira was crying in the bathroom as her mom tried to wash the sand off her dress. I tiptoed past them in the hallway. The door was closed, but I could hear them talking.

Maybe I should say something to make her feel better. But what?

"There, that doesn't look bad," Sheela Mausi said.

"Mom, it's a giant smudge!" Mira complained.

"You can hardly see it," Sheela Mausi replied. "Come on, let's go see what's cooking!"

They came out of the bathroom together, and I pretended to be searching for something on the floor so they wouldn't know I'd been listening in. After they passed me, I followed them into the kitchen.

Electric camping lanterns glowed from the counters, and Abu stood on a step stool near the stove, stirring a creamy red sauce that was bubbling. Dad watched over him while Ravi Mausa quickly chopped onions at another counter. We really were lucky that we could at least still cook even with no electricity. The sauce smelled so good!

"I think we're going to have a delicious meal," Sheela Mausi said, nudging Mira. "Don't you think so?"

Mira nodded.

"But what about the sparklers?" I asked, swallowing hard. "Will we be able to do those?"

I couldn't stand it if we couldn't light the sparklers in the backyard. That was the best part of Diwali! Last year Mira and I had so much fun waving the glowing sparks in the darkness.

"It's probably too rainy for sparklers," Dad said. "But for now, let's enjoy a snack." He put some hot pakoras on small plates for us. "Your pick of chutneys."

He had three different kinds lined up on the counter.

Mira took the tamarind sauce and mixed it with a spicy mango sauce. Then she dipped her pakora into it and munched. "Very good, Mausa."

Dad beamed. He was Mira's mausa, and her dad was my mausa, since our moms were sisters. As we snacked, I started to forget about the hurricane. Until Mom came in with a news report playing on her phone. It didn't sound good.

"... *Meteorologists are worried that the conditions might create a superstorm. Please stay tuned* ..."

Abu dropped the spoon he'd been using to stir, making curry fly everywhere. "A superstorm is coming! A superstorm is coming! A superstorm is coming!"

"It's only a maybe," Mom reminded my little brother.

Ravi Mausa picked up the spoon. "I thought hurricane season would be over by now."

"Sometimes they happen this late in the year," Dad said as he cleaned up the mess with an old rag.

Mom offered us each another pakora. "Did you know that Sheela Mausi has been working on weather-modeling computer software? Her program will help figure out where the hurricane will go and how big it will get."

"You didn't tell me you worked on that!" Mira said, poking Sheela Mausi.

"I most certainly did," Sheela Mausi said. "You just don't pay attention. You think my work is boring."

Mira rolled her eyes. "Yeah, because you're

always saying boring things about it. Blah, blah, numbers."

I had to laugh at that. "Just like my mom. Blah, blah, blah, atmospheric pressure."

We both giggled again. Grown-ups could take cool stuff and make it boring.

"You'll appreciate all the things we teach you someday," Mom said, ruffling my hair.

"Yeah, right, Mom," I answered.

"But what is a superstorm?" Mira asked.

Sheela Mausi popped a pakora into her mouth, chewed, and then answered. "Well, sometimes other types of weather systems—like thunderstorms or cold winds—meet the hurricane and make it even bigger and more destructive. That happened with Hurricane Sandy back in 2012, and it caused a lot of damage."

I didn't like the sound of that.

CHAPTER SEVEN
Time for Cardboard Box Magic

While the grown-ups kept talking, I slipped out and hurried down to the basement with my flashlight. Even if there was only a small chance that Hurricane Ruin-Everything would turn into a superstorm, this was still a total disaster of a Diwali.

I needed my stuffie! Professor Cheetah was on the shelf where I'd left her. I picked her up and gave her a hug, letting my tears fall. I'd had her since my second birthday, and she'd always been there for me when anything went wrong.

"This hurricane is ruining everything!" I wailed. "No rangoli. No sparklers. No power in the house. Diwali was the only thing that Mira was excited about doing with me, and now we can't even celebrate it!"

"So, obviously we should stop the hurricane," Professor Cheetah replied. She flicked her tail bossily. One thing about Professor Cheetah—she could be kind of a know-it-all. But right now I wanted her advice.

"How?" I asked.

She pointed at the cardboard box. "We'll turn our spaceship into a hurricane-hunting aircraft."

I thought about it. "That sounds dangerous. And . . . um . . . sort of fun?"

Professor Cheetah grinned her big cheetah grin. It was a little scary, honestly. Very toothy. But that was how she always looked when she had a big idea.

We got to work changing the cardboard box spaceship into a hurricane-hunting airplane. I put on new stickers for the plane's control panel.

We didn't need rocket parts anymore since we weren't going to outer space. Instead I added a more regular-looking speedometer to tell us how fast we were going. I also added an altimeter to tell us how high up we were, and all the other buttons and knobs we would need for steering the plane.

And I named our new aircraft with red marker: the SS *Cheetah*.

"Are we ready?" I asked.

Before Professor Cheetah could answer, Abu came running into the basement with his backpack. I could see a bunch of string cheese packets poking out of the side pocket.

"I need to pack! I need to pack!" he yelled, waving his hands frantically. "What should I bring to evacuate?"

"Were you listening to anything Mom and Sheela Mausi were saying?" I asked. "It's only a MAYBE. You don't need to pack."

"Yes I do!" Abu ran to put a bunch of toys into his already overstuffed backpack.

The door to the basement opened and shut again. Mira came shuffling down with her flashlight.

"Playing with a cardboard box again?" she asked, folding her arms.

It was time to remind Mira about all the magical kid power she'd forgotten. I climbed into the cardboard box with Professor Cheetah and put on my goggles. They were for swimming, but I was sure that they'd help out in windy, stormy weather, too.

"We're going on an adventure," I said. "Want to come?"

CHAPTER EIGHT
The Green Triangle of Power

Before Mira could answer, the room started to shake. The basement ceiling split wide open, but when I looked up, I didn't see the rest of the house. There was only the big gray sky. Plenty of wind and rain, too. It was time to press the most important button, a very special green triangle sticker on the control panel. It was a button that took the power of imagination and changed that energy into something amazing.

I carefully pushed it, and presto! The cardboard box expanded into a real airplane. I leaned out of the pilot's seat to look down the side, where SS *Cheetah* was still written in big red letters.

Professor Cheetah leaned over from the copilot's seat. She grinned her toothy cheetah grin. "Hello, Mira."

"Hi, Professor Cheetah." Mira waved back weakly. She seemed in shock.

"It's going to be a wild ride," Professor Cheetah purred.

Mira's eyes were big and round. "This must be a dream. Maybe I hit my head in the dark. That's the only explanation."

"We used to do this all the time, remember?" I said.

She bit her lip. "But we were just pretending."

"No, we weren't," I said. "It was always real. You just forgot about cardboard box magic."

"Hey, wait for me!" Abu pushed past Mira with his heavy backpack. "Don't worry, I've packed everything we need."

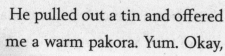

He pulled out a tin and offered me a warm pakora. Yum. Okay, maybe all his packing wasn't completely useless. Right beside him, Fluff Monster barked and wagged her tail. She put her paws up on the side of the airplane.

"This is too dangerous for you, Fluff," I said.

She let out a low growl to show she wasn't scared. Her tail wagged faster than the winds of a hurricane.

"Okay, okay, hop in," I said.

Fluff Monster was little, but she backed up, got a running start through Mira's legs, and jumped right into my lap.

"Good girl." I scratched her ears. "Mira, what about you?"

"I don't know." Mira looked nervously at the plane.

"Come on, who cares if this is a dream?" I

said—even though it definitely wasn't. "It's still more fun than staying here, right?"

"I guess so . . ." Mira slowly climbed into the backseat, shivering in the wind and rain.

I threw her a jacket and a pair of swim goggles. Abu had his own pair that he found in his backpack. He even had a doggie pair for Fluff Monster.

Once we were all ready for tough weather, I pushed the green triangle button again, and the plane took off, zooming into the big gray clouds.

CHAPTER NINE
The Monster's Eye

The ride was bumpy and rain splattered the windshield. Professor Cheetah was our navigator, which basically meant that she could be bossy about telling me which way to go.

Soon we were flying above Hurricane Ruin-Everything. From up here the sky was calm and the clouds of Ruin-Everything looked puffy and white. There was a hole in the middle of the hurricane, and the clouds around it looked like bubbles getting sucked down a giant bathtub drain.

"Why don't they look like normal gray storm clouds?" I asked Professor Cheetah.

"Storm clouds only look gray from underneath," she explained with her know-it-all voice. "They have more water inside them than other clouds, so it blocks more of the light from the sun when you're on the ground. From above, they still look white."

"That must be the eye," Mira said, pointing below. "It's the center of the hurricane."

"Cool." I'd almost forgotten my cousin was in the back, since she'd been so quiet during the trip. Probably trying to wake up from the dream she thought she was in.

Fluff Monster growled at the eye from my lap.

I laughed. "She still thinks she can scare the hurricane away."

"Do you have a better idea?" Mira asked.

"I'll come up with something," I promised.

"Uh-huh," Mira said. "I remember my teacher told us it's actually really calm inside the eye. Isn't that weird? But the clouds around the eye are the ones with the fastest winds and the most rain. That part is called the eyewall."

"Hurricanes have an eyeball?" Abu asked.

"No, eyeWALL."

"Are you sure?" Abu pressed his nose against

42

the plane window. "It looks like a monster's eye staring right at us!"

I rolled my eyes. "Don't tell me you think the hurricane is alive."

"It's a monster! It's a monster! It's a monster!" Abu yelled. "We need to give it treats. Like we do with Fluff Monster. Then it will be happy."

It was a silly idea, but sometimes there's no point arguing with five-year-olds. I pushed the green triangle button, and the top of the plane opened us up to the wind. We all put on our goggles and oxygen masks as we cruised along. Abu searched in his backpack, and then threw some snacks over the side: crackers with peanut butter, a few pakoras, dog biscuits, and even some impala-flavored chips. (Professor Cheetah's favorite.)

"Hey, I wanted those!" Professor Cheetah protested.

"What's an impala-flavored chip?" Mira asked, wrinkling her nose.

"They're for very refined tastes," Professor Cheetah said with a sniff. "I especially like the eastern savanna ones, but I suppose the southern ones are okay too."

She acted human in some ways, but Professor Cheetah still had her tastes from the African savanna life, where her kind liked to hunt gazelle, impala, and antelope. Her chips were a special order—not the kind you could find in a human grocery store!

Below us, the hurricane swallowed the snacks, but nothing really changed.

"So much for that idea," I said.

Suddenly Mira started bouncing in her seat excitedly. "Hey, look—there's another plane below us. And it's going straight into the hurricane!"

CHAPTER TEN
Junior Hurricane Hunters

I think it's a Hurricane Hunter," Mira said. "My mom told me that they fly all the way into the eye. The data they collect goes into Mom's computer modeling software to help scientists figure out where the hurricane is going and how bad it's going to be."

The plane had four big propellers on its wings. And sure enough, it was headed low over the ocean—right into the storm.

"Is it really safe to fly in there?" I asked.

Professor Cheetah cleared her throat, which

she always did before being a know-it-all. "The US government has been sending planes into hurricanes for more than seventy years. The first flight was the—"

"We don't have time for a history lesson!" Mira interrupted. "Quick! Let's follow it! If we want to stop the hurricane, we can probably learn a lot from a real Hurricane Hunter."

"I thought you were dreaming?" I asked her. She was finally getting into the adventure, but I wanted her to admit that this was real.

"Well, in my dream I think we should follow them," Mira said stubbornly. "Are you scared?"

So much for admitting anything.

"Of course I'm not scared," I said. "It was my idea to stop the hurricane, wasn't it?"

"Actually, it was mine," Professor Cheetah argued.

I huffed. "Okay, it was my idea second, then!"

I hit the lever to swoop down to the other plane. Seeing the hurricane from above hadn't seemed too scary, but from down here the storm

looked a lot worse. Dark and frightening and way too big for us to stop. But we had to try! Or there might not be any Diwali to celebrate tonight.

We pulled alongside the Hurricane Hunter. Through the front window we could see three people seated in a row. They were staring at us with surprised looks.

The person in the pilot's seat grabbed the radio, and a woman's voice came on our speaker. "Hello, can you hear us? This is Joanna, pilot of this here Hurricane Hunter. Please identify your aircraft and destination. Over."

"What should I say?" I asked my crew.

Mira leaned forward. "Um . . . you could tell them we're Hurricane Hunters in training?"

"Ooh, I hadn't thought of that," I said. "Good idea."

I picked up our radio.

"Yes, we can hear you," I said nervously. "We are the . . . uh . . . SS *Cheetah*. We're . . . um . . . a new Hurricane Hunter team. We're here to train with you. Over."

"No offense, but you sound like a bunch of kids," Pilot Joanna said, peering through the window. "And is that a dog with you? And . . . a jaguar? Over."

I glanced back at Mira again. "Psst. What now?"

"Just tell them we look young!" she whispered. "They probably can't see us that well from way over there anyway."

I didn't know if that would work, but I didn't have anything to lose. I pushed the talk button on the radio again.

"Um . . . we're not kids! We just look young!" I fibbed. "The puppy is, um, our mascot. And, um, that's just a picture of a cheetah. Not a jaguar. It's probably hard to tell through the plane window. Over."

I rolled my eyes. Grown-ups never seemed to know the different big cats, for some reason. Even though cheetahs had completely different spots than jaguars.

"Nobody told me about any training program,"

Joanna muttered. "But you just follow our lead. Got it? We're about to head into the storm. We'll need to take measurements inside the hurricane at different points. It's about three hundred miles across, so we've got a lot of air to cover."

Wow, she actually believed me! "Roger that. We'll just follow you, then. Over."

"Great," Joanna said. "Stick with us and stay safe. Over."

I could see her shaking her head and saying something to her copilot and other team members.

"We're doing this!" I said excitedly.

"In a dream," Mira said.

I shook my head before closing the top again so we'd be more protected. We followed the Hurricane Hunter into the big scary hurricane, flying low over the ocean. Soon the clouds were thick around us, like fog. Rain splattered our windshield. The wind screamed. Thunder crackled and lighting flashed outside. Mira jumped.

"Still think this is a dream?" I asked her.

CHAPTER ELEVEN
Feeding the Monster

The Hurricane Hunter dropped some kind of cylinder out the bottom of their plane. It was attached to its own small parachute.

"See?" Abu said. "They're trying to feed the monster too."

"I don't think that's what they're doing," I said, then spoke into the radio. "What was that? Over."

"They really haven't told you much about our mission, huh?" Joanna said. "That was a dropsonde. It's a special instrument that will measure things like temperature, humidity, and wind speed at different altitudes."

"'Altitude' means 'height,'" Professor Cheetah said.

"I *know* that," I returned. "I made the altimeter to measure how high we are, remember?"

Professor Cheetah's whiskers twitched. "And I made it actually work."

Such a know-it-all! At least she was a good mechanic.

"We'll release about twenty of them in different parts of the hurricane," Joanna continued. "That information gets sent back to the weather-forecasting station, where computer models will try to predict where the hurricane is going. It's really important to get the best data so the experts can decide who needs to evacuate. Over."

"Oh yeah, I knew about dropsondes—obviously," I replied. "To collect info about the hurricane. Cool. What's next? Over."

"We'll fly in a triangle to cover different parts of the hurricane. That will help us locate the center of the storm. Then we'll head in, through the eyewall. Things will get pretty bumpy! And you won't be able to see much, so keep an eye on your altimeter. If you go too high or low, your aircraft could lose control. So stay steady, about where we are now. Got it, kid? Over."

That sounded scary, but I wasn't going to admit that. "Got it. And don't call me a kid. Over."

"No problem, kid. Over."

I rolled my eyes.

Our altimeter said we were about ten thousand feet high. I tried to stay at the same level as we pushed forward. Things around our plane got darker and rainier, and it was hard to see the Hurricane Hunter. But we could follow it on the radar, which I knew sent particles in the air to find out where things were. The particles would hit the Hurricane Hunter and then bounce back to us. The radar could then figure out how far away they were.

We followed them, going in a triangle pattern first. Then we headed inward, to the eye.

"We're punching into the eyewall," the pilot said over the radio. "Make sure you're strapped in and hang on! Over."

CHAPTER TWELVE
Punching into the Eyewall

I pulled Fluff Monster behind the seat belt with me. We were smooshed, but it was safer. We couldn't see anything outside, with the rain smashing against the windows. It was like driving through a car wash. A gust of air pushed us down, and then another gust pushed us up. We bounced hard a few times.

"Ahhhh!" I screamed.

"Ahhhh!" Mira screamed. "This dream is turning into a nightmare!"

"Woof! Woof! Woof!" Fluff Monster barked and then growled at Ruin-Everything. I wished her growling really could scare it away, but so far the hurricane was winning.

"Where's the eyeball?" Abu asked.

"It's an eyewall!" Mira and I both yelled at him at the same time.

Munch, munch, munch. Abu was a loud chewer and apparently not worried about the fact that our plane might fall apart at any second.

"Stay calm," Professor Cheetah yelled over the wind. "Slow down the plane! We're going too fast."

Another gust of wind pushed us up some more, and things got even bumpier.

"Remember to try to stay at ten thousand feet!" shouted Professor Cheetah. The wind roared around us.

"I'm trying!" I retorted. "The wind keeps pushing the plane up and down!"

"Yes," Professor Cheetah said, "those are updrafts and downdrafts of air. Warm air rises up from the ocean and then cools and makes thunderclouds, which release rain and push air downward. The winds stir the warm air below, and surrounding warm air gets sucked into the system. That causes more water vapor to form from the warm water below. This cycle keeps the hurricane going."

Bump. Thump. Creak.

"Now we're heading into the eye," Joanna said over the radio. "Veer right to gently leave the eye-wall winds. Got it, kid? Over."

"What the heck does 'veer right' mean?" I muttered.

Mira shrugged. "Go right?"

"Slowly!" Professor Cheetah added.

But it was too late. I had already swung my steering wheel to the right, and we shot forward really fast.

"Ahhhh!" we all screamed again. Even Abu this time. His half-eaten cheese stick went flying and bonked me on the back of the head.

CHAPTER THIRTEEN
The Calm inside the Storm

A second later we were in a place where we could actually see around us.

"We're in the eye!" Mira said excitedly. "I can't believe we're actually in the middle of the hurricane. And it's so calm here."

She was right. It was beautiful. The eyewall surrounded us, but from here it didn't look scary. The clouds looked puffy and white, like they had from above the hurricane. Down below the SS *Cheetah*, I could see all the way to the blue ocean. It was like we were in a cylinder. The Hurricane Hunter released another dropsonde, and the parachute helped slow it down. I guessed it could take more measurements that way before it fell into the ocean.

Mira took off her seat belt. And then my older cousin—the one who was too cool for cardboard boxes and stuffies and thought this was a dream—reached out and shook Professor Cheetah's paw. "Great job navigating."

Fluff Monster woofed, and Mira petted her. "And great job scaring that mean rain and wind, Fluff." She turned to my little brother. "Who

knows, Abu? Maybe feeding the hurricane really is a good idea."

"Snacks help everything." Abu offered Mira a cheese stick, and she took it.

Mira didn't say anything about me, though. Whatever. I had a job to do.

"Come in, Hurricane Hunter. What's next?" I asked on the radio. "Over."

"We're going to try to find the exact center of the hurricane," Joanna said. "That's really important information for the computer models. Over."

"Why haven't you figured out a way to actually

stop the hurricane?" I asked. "Shouldn't scientists be working on that? Over."

The pilot laughed through the radio. She actually laughed at me! How rude.

"Well, back in the 1960s the government created Project STORMFURY—a program where they actually did try to stop hurricanes. But the project never worked. Turns out humans can't really control the weather. Over."

I glared at the radio. "What do you mean? We've invented so many great things! And we're just giving up on stopping hurricanes? Over."

"Hey, kid," the pilot said. "I don't make the rules. Maybe you can change their minds. Over."

"Okay, maybe I will," I said. "Over."

I put away the radio and dropped my head against the dash. Even the Hurricane Hunters thought my mission was impossible. What was I going to do?

Mira reached out and patted my shoulder. "Maybe this is a job for kids, not adults. After all, they barely have any imagination."

I turned to face her. "Just adults?"

Mira paused. "Okay, I know I've been giving you a hard time. But I believe you. This is real."

I whooped and hollered with excitement. Mira believed me! Abu also cheered, and Professor Cheetah purred.

Fluff Monster said, "Arf! Arf! Arf!"

She was so excited, her tail wagging so hard . . . that it hit one of the levers on the dash!

Suddenly we were shooting way, way down!

CHAPTER FOURTEEN
Bumptastic

Ack!" I yelled as I totally lost control of the plane.
Fluff Monster got thrown out from under the seat
belt.

"Don't worry, I've got her," Mira said, pulling
Fluff into her lap.

"Woof!" barked Fluff Monster.

The SS *Cheetah* was back in the eyewall.
Only this time we had dropped much lower. And
Joanna was right—there was a lot more wind down
here. We were spinning as if we were in a tornado.

Wind whacked us all over the place as if it were a tennis racket and we were the ball.

I tried to slow us down, but the hurricane was too strong and none of my controls or levers could fight against it. Big gusts of wind batted us around.

"Stop bumping! Stop bumping! Stop bumping!" Abu yelled.

"I'm trying!" I yelled back.

"Maybe it's like quicksand," Mira said. "It gets worse the more you struggle. So you need to do less, not more. Stop trying to fight it."

"I concur with this plan," Professor Cheetah said. Whatever "concur" meant. Probably "agree."

"Stop fighting! Stop fighting! Stop fighting!" Abu yelled.

I couldn't think of anything better to do, so I listened. Instead of trying to fight against the powerful wind, I tried to ride it, like a surfer on waves. At first we were still getting beaten up by the hurricane, but slowly the ride became smoother. Just like Mira had said.

Riding the wind was actually a very fun feeling. Soon we were out of the eyewall. There was still fog surrounding us, but not as thick.

"Great job," Mira said, grinning.

I grinned back. Older cousins weren't easy to impress!

We spotted the Hurricane Hunter ahead.

"That was some reckless flying," Joanna said over the radio, "but I'm glad you regained control. Not bad, Junior Hurricane Hunter. Over."

My heart swelled with pride. I'd impressed my older cousin *and* we were junior Hurricane Hunters! Would we get a badge or something? Probably not, since we were lying about being in a training program. But still. It was pretty cool that we'd impressed a real-life Hurricane Hunter pilot.

"Thanks," I said. "Are you done with your work? Over."

"Nope," Joanna said. "We'll be working around the clock for the next few days. But we're heading back to base to refuel. What about you kids—I mean, what about you Hurricane Hunters in training? Over."

"Our training time is up for today," I answered. "But . . . where would we learn more about Project STORMFURY? Over."

"Let's see. There's a guy you could talk to, one of the few people who still think we can actually change the weather," Joanna said. "His name is Ross Herman, and he's in Wyoming, at the National Center for Atmospheric Research Supercomputing Center. But don't you need to report to base now? Over."

"Um, yes," I said. "We're totally going to report to base. Maybe we'll see you there! Over."

CHAPTER FIFTEEN
Abu and the High-Tech Backpack

I turned to my crew. "What do you think? Should we talk to this Ross Herman guy? Or go back to the basement?"

"Ross Herman!" said Abu.

"I concur," said Professor Cheetah.

"Woof!" agreed Fluff Monster.

I looked back at Mira. "What do you think? Or should we wake up from this dream?"

"It's not a dream," Mira said firmly. "And we

need to go to Wyoming. We can do this. *You* can do this, Sejal."

My heart felt really big right then. My eyes watered. But they were good tears, not bad ones.

Munch. Munch. Munch.

Abu was now crunching on some peanut butter crackers.

"I'm surprised you have any of those left after feeding Ruin-Everything," I said.

"Mrfllen," Abu replied.

He passed me his backpack, which was still overflowing with all kinds of snacks. Professor Cheetah took over flying while I rummaged for yummy treats. The more I looked, the more I found. I passed some doggie biscuits to Fluff Monster.

"How did you fit all this?" I pulled out a granola bar, a sugar cookie, a water bottle, and carrot sticks for myself.

"It's my extra-deep backpack. Professor Cheetah invented it," said Abu. "It fits more than you think, huh?"

Abu sure was full of surprises.

"Very high-tech," Professor Cheetah said. "It required a lot of skill."

I leaned way into the backpack, and it felt like I might tumble in, like there was a whole big basement in there. Definitely not an ordinary backpack. I handed it to Mira, who pulled out an applesauce cup, a chocolate chip cookie, and her own water bottle. Then she found more impala-flavored chips and a gazelle soda for Professor Cheetah.

"Don't mind if I do!" Professor Cheetah grinned her toothy cheetah grin.

With snacks to give us energy and Professor Cheetah's amazing navigator skills, it wasn't long before we landed the SS *Cheetah* in a grassy area behind the Supercomputing Center. When I pushed the special green triangle button, our plane turned back into the cardboard box. Fluff Monster was excited to have a potty break, and ran around in circles before doing her business.

After hiding the cardboard box in the bushes,

we walked around to the main entrance in the front. The building in the back was boring and gray with hardly any windows, but the front had a shiny circular part with big windows. The sign said, NCAR-WYOMING SUPERCOMPUTING CENTER.

There was a giant cowboy boot statue just outside the door. It had lots of hurricanes painted all over it—with a Hurricane Hunter flying into one of them!

"I can't believe we did that," I said. Suddenly it felt like a dream even to me. Earlier today I'd been certain we could stop the hurricane. But now that I'd seen it myself, I wasn't so sure.

"It was pretty awesome!" Mira said.

I hugged her. "Thanks for coming with me."

She hugged me back. "Thanks for reminding me about cardboard box magic."

Her hug felt like the best thing in the world. With Mira's help, we were unstoppable. Even Fluff Monster barked her approval.

"Um, they probably don't allow dogs," Mira pointed out.

"Don't worry," said Abu. "She'll fit in here." He put her inside his backpack and left it unzipped for air. "Be good," he said to her.

"Arf! Arf! Arf!" Fluff Monster responded.

"And quiet," he told her.

"Arf!" she said in a much quieter tone.

"Good doggie."

I couldn't believe Fluff actually listened to him. She always listened to everyone except me. But then she poked her head out, licked me like she knew I was thinking of her, and settled back into the backpack.

CHAPTER SIXTEEN
Supercomputers, Arfs, and Grumpy Ross Herman

As we walked into the lobby, Professor Cheetah went quiet again too, so I picked her up and held her like she was a regular toy. A woman wearing a "SCIENCE IS COOL!" T-shirt just like mine smiled at us.

"Nice shirt," she said to me.

"Thanks." I kept my arms down so no one would see the hole in the armpit.

"Welcome!" she continued. "I'm Liz. Are you here to see our famous supercomputer, Derecho?"

"Derecho?" Mira asked. "Isn't that a kind of storm? We've been learning about weather at school."

"Yes, it is!" Liz said. "It's a very dangerous type of windstorm. But it's also the name of our supercomputer. We use it for forecasting weather."

"Actually," I said, "we're here to see a man named Ross Herman? We want to learn about Project STORMFURY and how to stop a hurricane."

Liz lost her smile. "Ross Herman? Are you sure? He's pretty grumpy and doesn't like to talk to visitors."

"We have to see him!" I said. "It's really important!"

"Arf!" Fluff agreed.

"What was that?" Liz looked at us suspiciously. "Dogs aren't allowed in here, except service animals."

"Um, that was just my little brother," I said. "He likes to pretend he's a dog sometimes."

Abu smiled and said, "Arf! Arf!"

He sounded exactly like Fluff Monster.

Liz got her smile back. "That's cute. Would you like a biscuit, little doggie?" She offered him a cookie, which Abu happily munched on.

"You can each have one." She handed cookies to me and Mira, too. "Okay, I'll show you to Ross's office, and you can see Derecho along the way."

"Thanks," I said.

"Arf!" said either Fluff Monster or Abu. I honestly wasn't sure which.

The supercomputer Derecho looked like a bunch of black refrigerators lined up in rows.

"That's just one computer? Taking up the whole entire room?" Mira asked. "Seriously?"

"You got it," Liz said. "That's a lot of computer power in there. Now, here we are at Ross's office."

She knocked on the door.

"Who is it?" a grumpy voice said from the other side.

"Dr. Herman, you have some visitors," Liz replied. "They're just kids, so try to be nice."

"Kids?" the man said. "I don't have time for kids! I'm busy."

"Please, sir," I said through the door. "We're really interested in your research."

"Go write your book report somewhere else."

Liz shrugged. "I told you he was grumpy. I can show you around some more, though."

"No, we're not leaving!" I said loudly enough

that I was sure Grumpy Ross could hear me from inside his office.

"Yes, you are!" he answered back.

Meanwhile, Abu sat down in the hallway and pulled out the tin of pakoras, paper plates, and three kinds of chutneys from the high-tech backpack.

"Ooh, that looks amazing," Liz said.

"Try some," Abu said. "My dad's recipe."

Liz munched for a while, and a few minutes later Ross Herman's door opened.

"Okay, what is that delicious smell?"

CHAPTER SEVENTEEN
The Importance of Snacks

After Dr. Herman had eaten most of the pakoras, he seemed to be in a much better mood. He let us into his office. Abu, Mira, and I squeezed together on a small sofa. Abu pretended to "Arf!" whenever Fluff Monster called from inside his backpack. She was probably bored in there. Professor Cheetah stayed in her silent ordinary-stuffie mode.

"So you want to change the weather, huh?" Dr. Herman asked from behind his desk.

"We want to stop Hurricane Ruin-Everything right now!" I said, leaning forward.

"Hurricane Ruin-Everything, huh?" he said. "We've tried controlling hurricanes before but haven't had much luck."

"Project STORMFURY, right?" I asked, remembering what Pilot Joanna had told us.

He smiled. "Looks like you know your stuff, young lady. Yes, Project STORMFURY was a government program in the 1960s and '70s. It was based on the idea of cloud seeding. That means we were trying to create more rain. They thought if the clouds grew faster and there was more rain in the hurricane, it would get weaker. Maybe even fizzle into just a rainstorm. You see, only certain things can keep the hurricane powerful and strong."

"What kind of things?" asked Mira.

"All hurricanes are powered by warm water and warm temperatures. The warm water evaporates—that means it turns from liquid water into the kind of water vapor that makes clouds. And those clouds make thunderstorms. Most thunderstorms just give some rain and it's no big deal."

"Arf!" Fluff complained again.

Dr. Herman looked at Abu suspiciously, so Abu said, "Arf!"

"So what happens with hurricanes that makes them stronger?" I asked quickly to distract him.

It seemed to work because Dr. Herman kept talking. "Basically, with a hurricane system, a cycle starts that's hard to stop once it gets going. Warm air gets sucked in under the clouds, which then causes the warm water below to evaporate. That makes even more thunderclouds. Because of the spinning of the Earth, the storm starts spinning too. The spinning sucks in even more warm air. The cycle continues with the warm air and the warm water below feeding the hurricane and making it strong."

Abu's eyes widened. "See? The hurricane really is hungry."

"Yes, it's quite a monster," Ross said. "But not the usual kind. With Project STORMFURY, they thought that extra rain from the clouds would cool down the air below and weaken the system."

"So why didn't it work?" I asked.

"Well," Dr. Herman said, "they released special chemicals that were supposed to stick to tiny cold water particles in the clouds to make them heavy with extra rain. But we think now that there weren't enough cold water particles in the first place in a hurricane. The reason that the project went on so long was because it's hard to tell if the hurricanes eventually fizzled on their own or because of what we were doing."

My shoulders slumped. "So now what? They're really not even going to try to stop hurricanes anymore?"

"Actually," said Dr. Herman, "I'm trying! I do a lot of computer modeling here on Derecho. That means I use computers to try to figure out the behaviors of hurricanes."

"Like your mom!" I said to Mira, who nodded.

"Oh?" Dr. Herman smiled. "Sounds like you've got some scientists in the family."

"Yes, we do!" Mira and I said at the same time. And then we laughed.

"Glad to hear it!" Dr. Herman said. "I've learned that if you change just a few things about a hurricane—even just a little bit—it loses its strength. One idea I had was that we could put oil on the ocean water to stop it from evaporating. That would kill the cycle."

"Oil? Gross," I said. "That would be bad for the ocean."

"There are some kinds of biodegradable oils we could use," Dr. Herman said, "but so far we haven't been able to spread them enough for it to work."

I thought hard about everything he'd told me. "You said hurricanes are powered by warm water. So what if we drop an iceberg into the ocean? Then it would be cold underneath."

Ross nodded. "Yes, that's a great idea. The

problem is transporting a big enough iceberg to make a difference. We don't know how to do it."

I glanced at Professor Cheetah. She was in her quiet-around-adults mood. But I had a feeling she might have an idea.

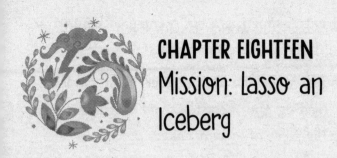

CHAPTER EIGHTEEN
Mission: lasso an Iceberg

Ross Herman said there was no way to transport a giant iceberg. But that's the thing about cardboard boxes. They're powered by imagination, and that's no small thing.

"Is this really gonna work? We won't have to evacuate?" Abu asked, looking down over the side of the plane as we flew north. Professor Cheetah had attached a giant harness below the plane—a bunch of straps that would carry the iceberg.

"*Of course* it'll work," I said. Even though I wasn't sure at all.

"It's just the same as your idea," Mira added. "We're feeding the monster. And the monster wants a big piece of iceberg cake."

Abu's eyes widened. "Oh. OH. OH. Yes, it is my idea!"

He smiled, looking very proud of himself.

Mira high-fived me. "This is going to be so awesome."

If Mira thought it would work, it had to. Right?

We passed over the cold front and a different storm along the coast. Scientists were worried these weather systems would bump into Hurricane Ruin-Everything. If they hit each other, Ruin-Everything *might* fizzle out—or it *might* turn into a superstorm that could destroy even more stuff than a regular hurricane! It was annoying that those computer models that Sheela Mausi had worked on couldn't tell us which one of those things would happen.

"Do you see any good ones?" I asked when we reached Greenland.

"We'll need an especially big one to cool the water enough to stop the hurricane," Professor Cheetah said.

"That one looks pretty huge," Mira said.

It did look big. Like a whole town could live there. Maybe even a city.

"That's way too big for our harness, isn't it?" I asked.

Professor Cheetah considered. "I think we can handle it."

We landed in the middle of the iceberg and jumped out. The ice was slick, and our feet slid a little. I almost fell. Mira actually did fall.

She got a big grin on her face. "Race you down!"

And then she sledded down the side of the iceberg on her butt. It looked pretty fun!

"We're sledding! We're sledding! We're sledding!" yelled Abu as he slid down behind her.

"Arf!" said Fluff Monster, who started spinning and sliding behind them.

I looked at Professor Cheetah. "Um, do you need help or something?"

Professor Cheetah grinned. "Don't worry, I got this."

So, I slid down the ice too.

"Woo-hoo!" I yelled. It was like being at a water park, but better. It was an ice park, and it was all ours.

CHAPTER NINETEEN
Unstoppable Kid Power

I crashed into Mira at the bottom. Luckily, we didn't fall off the iceberg into the freezing water.

"You know, hanging out with you is pretty fun," Mira said.

OH MY GOSH. My older cousin—who was too cool for stuffies and cardboard boxes just a few hours ago—actually thought I was fun! Maybe we didn't need rangoli and sparklers to be friends after all. I hugged her, hard.

Soon Professor Cheetah had attached the

harness to the iceberg, and we all scrambled back into the plane. I pulled the throttle up to full power. Could we really lift something as big as this iceberg? It was impossible for any ordinary plane, of course. But we had cardboard box power. We had kid power. We had imagination power.

The plane fought to fly up, to lift the impossibly big iceberg. I squeezed my eyes shut.

"We need to do this!" I screamed.

"You can do it, SS *Cheetah*," Mira shouted.

"Go, go, go!" Abu added between munches of a cheese stick.

"Arf! Arf! Arf!" barked Fluff Monster.

And we did it! The power of imagination worked—the plane lifted the huge iceberg out of the water. It was amazing!

"Go, kid power!" Mira said, high-fiving me.

I felt unstoppable. We were stronger than a hurricane. As we headed back south over the Atlantic, I tuned into the radio news.

"*The cold-weather air currents have now*

collided with the hurricane, pushing it around so it's unpredictable where it will go. Stand by for our full report—"

Mira reached across me and switched it off. "Nothing's changed. They still don't know if Hurricane Ruin-Everything will turn into a super-storm or where it will go. But we know what we have to do."

"Yes, we do," I agreed.

The rest of the ride to the hurricane was quiet. Abu fell asleep with a comic book on his face. Fluff took a little nap too, her legs twitching. She was probably dreaming about chasing squirrels. Professor Cheetah was muttering something to herself as she made calculations.

"We're here," I said when we reached the gray clouds of Hurricane Ruin-Everything. I didn't see the Hurricane Hunter plane anywhere. That was good—they probably wouldn't believe what we were about to do.

This time we knew what to expect when we flew into the eyewall. The weight of the iceberg kept us steadier than before, since air drafts weren't able to bounce us up and down. Then we made it into Hurricane Ruin-Everything's eye.

"Drop it here," Mira said.

"No, we need to find the exact center of the hurricane for the best results," Professor Cheetah argued. "Luckily, the Hurricane Hunter already reported it to the National Hurricane Center, and the new computer models will tell us where to go."

I followed her instructions to where the exact center was.

"Now!" she said.

I pushed the red circle button to release the iceberg. It dropped into the water with a gigantic splash.

CHAPTER TWENTY
Mission Accomplished?

"Did it work?" Abu asked.

"I don't know," I answered. I was hoping I'd see something, anything that would mean the storm was calming down.

"The eyewall pretty much looks the same," Mira said. "It doesn't look like anything has changed."

I moaned. "But we worked so hard and dropped a giant iceberg. It has to work!"

Professor Cheetah rubbed my back gently with her furry paw. "It will take a while for that much ice to melt," she purred. "There's still hope. We just have to wait."

She really was the smartest and best of all my stuffies. I just hoped she was right.

The iceberg had *seemed* so big. But now, inside the eye of the huge hurricane, I wasn't so sure. Compared to this storm, maybe the iceberg was nothing. I had a bad feeling that maybe we hadn't helped at all. Maybe humans couldn't control forces this big.

Mira touched my shoulder. "Look, we tried. I'm proud of us. I'm proud of *you*, Sejal. But now it's time to go home."

Home.

Where Mom and Dad and Ravi Mausa and Sheela Mausi were waiting for us. Dad was probably done cooking by now. Unless . . . they'd been told to evacuate. What if they weren't there by the time we got back?

"Okay," I said. "We'll go home."

Fluff Monster licked my face. She knew it was the right thing to do, too.

We punched back into the eyewall. It was just as bumpy as ever. We still couldn't see a thing. We didn't have all the measuring instruments the Hurricane Hunter did, so I didn't know how fast the winds were blowing. Probably just as fast as last time. But now I knew how to handle the jolts and the wind batting at us like an angry cat playing with a ball of yarn. We made it out the other side, and not much later we landed back inside my basement.

The lights were still out and the basement was dark.

CHAPTER TWENTY-ONE
A Cozy Feast

We climbed out of the airplane, which had transformed back into a cardboard box with stickers on it. I was nervous.

"What if they evacuated?" I whispered.

Mira rubbed my shoulders. "They wouldn't have left without us."

"But what if they had to?"

But then we heard footsteps upstairs. The basement door swung open.

"SAY-JULL! MEE-RAH!" Mom called.

91

I'd never been so excited to hear her voice. I grabbed my flashlight and ran up the steps, Abu and Mira just behind me. Fluff Monster woofed and beat me to Mom, who rubbed her behind the ears.

"I'm glad you're still here." I said, squishing against Mom in a big hug.

She smiled. "Of course I'm here. You kids sure have been keeping yourselves busy! Not a peep from any of you!"

"Oh, that's us all right." Mira winked at me. "Just playing quietly in the basement. We definitely didn't do anything else."

"Definitely not," I agreed.

"Come on," Mom said. "Dinner's ready."

The dining room looked cozy and perfect, with candles all around. On the table there was a huge Diwali feast waiting for us: chole, bhature, baingan bharta, mattar paneer, saag, aloo gobi, sabjee vindaloo, and even crisp pani poories! My mouth watered even though I'd snacked plenty with Abu's Limitless Backpack. Stopping hurricanes gave you a big appetite, I guessed.

"I'll be right back!" I said, and ran to my bedroom. Mom had left a pretty lehenga for me, lying on the bottom bunk of my bed. I switched out of my "SCIENCE IS COOL!" T-shirt to the lehenga quickly and looked in the mirror. My hair was sticking up all over the place like I'd flown right through a hurricane, but other than that, I looked pretty good.

CHAPTER TWENTY-TWO
Light over Darkness, Take Two

When I came back into the dining room, Fluff Monster was under the table sniffing for crumbs and Abu was sneaking some poori bits to her.

"Sit next to me!" Mira said, pointing at the chair that had been left empty.

Sheela Mausi started dumping vindaloo onto my plate, and Mom gave me a huge heaping of mattar paneer. Ravi Mausa piled some chole and bhature on, and Dad gave me all the pani poori fixings. The grown-ups were definitely not going to let me go hungry, and I was glad.

Just as I started to take an enormous bite, the lights flickered from the chandelier over the table.

They flickered one more time . . .

And then they were on!

We all started clapping.

"Oh, wonderful!" Sheela Mausi exclaimed.

"Yay! Yay! Yay!" Abu yelled.

He ran around the dining room table in circles, Fluff dashing after him. After a second I laughed and joined him. Then so did Mira. We ran and screamed with joy and danced around the table. I thought the grown-ups would tell us to calm down, but instead Dad got up and joined us. Then Mom, Sheela Mausi, and Ravi Mausa did too. When we finally got tired, we sat down and ate until we were totally stuffed, and then told lots of silly jokes and laughed so much our stomachs hurt.

When we got quiet, Mom put on the news to check on Hurricane Ruin-Everything.

". . . It seems the hurricane's strength died down before it had a chance to hit land. Experts are puzzled, though they're speculating that it may have hit some cold currents in the ocean. Very lucky for us . . ."

My eyes were wide. Cold currents? Did that mean what I thought it did?

Mira winked at me and whispered, "Guess that iceberg did the trick!"

I smiled. "Iceberg? What iceberg? I think you were dreaming."

She laughed. "Yeah, right, there's no way I could dream an adventure that big!"

After dinner, the rain had gone away too. We lit sparklers in the driveway and Ravi Mausa put on some bhangra music and the grown-ups brought out the dessert. We ate too many sweets and laughed some more. It was the best Diwali ever, just like I'd hoped.

Hurricane Ruin-Everything hadn't ruined anything. Light had won over darkness, like it was supposed to. And Mira even believed in cardboard box magic again.

At bedtime she climbed up to the top bunk in my room. I turned out the light and got under the covers in the bottom bunk.

"Great job navigating today," I whispered to Professor Cheetah.

Then a stuffed unicorn face appeared upside down from the top bunk.

"Next time, don't forget to take me on the adventure!" Mr. Sparkles said. "I can't believe I was stuck in Mira's suitcase all day. I missed all the fun."

I giggled. "Oh, er . . . sorry."

Mira giggled too. "Sorry, Mr. Sparkles. Next time, for sure."

AUTHOR'S NOTE

Every year hurricanes form over the Atlantic Ocean in tropical waters. Sometimes they lose their strength as they travel and there might not be much damage. Other times they can cause a lot of flooding and destruction. They can injure people and even cause many deaths. It's possible that climate change is making hurricanes stronger and more frequent. That's why it's important for us to predict where a hurricane is going, so people can evacuate dangerous areas and stay safe.

Hurricane Hunters are a real part of the US Air Force Reserves, and they actually do fly straight into hurricanes to gather data that will go into our computer models. Those models help tell us where a hurricane is going, and how much damage it might cause. Hurricane Hunters even fly right through the eyewall and into the eye of the storm.

Can we actually control hurricanes? Right

now the answer is no. Project STORMFURY was a real government project in the 1960s, in which planes were flown into hurricanes to try to change the way the hurricane clouds formed, by releasing silver iodide particles. But it wasn't clear that these attempts were actually making a difference, and in 1971, Project STORMFURY flew its last mission. These days most efforts are focused on predicting hurricanes and understanding them better, rather than trying to stop them. But you never know when there might be a new scientific breakthrough!

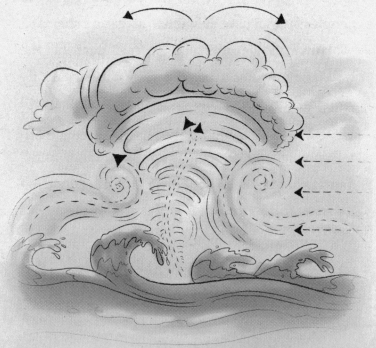

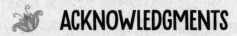 # ACKNOWLEDGMENTS

I owe this book to my kiddo, Commander B, the cardboard box explorer in my life with a beloved stuffed cheetah. Thanks for telling me the first cool science fact that sparked the Sejal series. Every day, your spunk, humor, and inner sparkle light up my life.

Penny Moore, you're a rockstar agent! I'm incredibly thankful for your belief in the importance of stories featuring BIPOC kids doing all kinds of things. Alyson Heller, I'm so grateful to get to work with such a fabulous editor who loves to promote marginalized voices. Abira Das: I was blown away by your gorgeous illustrations! Thank you so much for bringing the characters to life on the cover and with the interior art.

Thanks also Kristin Gilson, Valerie Garfield, Anna Jarzab, Olivia Ritchie, Heather Palisi, Amelia Jenkins, Anna Elling, Bezawit Yohannes, and the rest of the team at Aladdin for all your hard work. A shout out to the Aevitas Creative Management team as well, including the interns!

Thank you to my fantastic critique group for your insights for my early chapters: Flor Salcedo, S. Isabelle, Linda Cheng, Michele Bacon, and Candace Buford. I'm also grateful for Paul Decker, Zoe Fisher, and the rest of our writing meetup for reading an even earlier iteration of *Sejal*.

Thanks Cleo: cookies-and-cream colored Havanese are obviously the best.

To my husband: I love that you always say "this is your best work yet" to everything I write. You inspire me, too.

Cheers to the parents, teachers, librarians, booksellers, and caregivers who seek out diverse reading for kids. And to the kiddos who are ready to conquer new worlds: never forget kid power and the magic of a cardboard box!

Don't miss Sejal's next adventure!

Sejal Sinha

Swims with Sea Dragons

BY MAYA PRASAD ★ ILLUSTRATED BY ABIRA DAS

The best part about school projects is definitely the glitter.

I was working on a poster for my ocean creatures presentation on the dining room table, and I added another dash of red glitter, just to make the tummy of my immortal jellyfish look extra bright.

"Can I help?" asked my five-year-old little brother, Abu.

"No way," I said. "This needs to be perfect."

Abu made a pouty face, and then snatched the glitter bottle.

"Stay away!" I said.

He got an evil-little-brother look. The next thing I knew, a glitter bomb exploded all over us!

Our cookies-and-cream-colored Havanese puppy, Fluff Monster, yapped and ran in circles in the cloud of red sparkles. It got all over her fur. All over my hair. All over Abu the most. He looked like he was made of sparkly fire.

Mom came in to see what Fluff Monster was barking about. She took one look at Abu, and just shook her head. I waited for her to get super mad but instead she laughed. "New look you're trying out?"

Abu grinned and twirled. "Yeah, do I look good?"

"Very good," Mom said. But she also fixed him with a stern look and held out her hand.

He stopped twirling and gave her the glitter shaker.

"Thank you," Mom said.

I rolled my eyes because it seemed like Abu never got into trouble for anything. But Mom would probably yell at me for making a mess on the table.

She came over to look at my poster. "Wow, Sejal! Your project is coming out so nicely. I wish I could live forever like the immortal jellyfish!"

Phew. She was smiling at least. Maybe her latest experiments at her science lab had been going well or something.

"Sorry about the mess on the dining table," I said, "but Fluff Monster kept stealing my markers when I tried to work on it in the basement."

I loved Fluff, but she could definitely be naughty sometimes. And she really liked stealing anything that was stick-shaped, like pencils or markers. The dining table was too high for her to reach, though.

Mom rubbed my shoulders. "It's okay. Not like we're expecting anyone today."

"Nope, just a normal evening!" Dad said cheerfully from kitchen. "We can eat dinner on the kitchen island."

I noticed he was wearing his favorite frilly apron and was stirring a big pot with lots of steam coming out. Something smelled good, but I'd been so busy working on my project that I hadn't paid attention until right now.

Just then, Fluff Monster started barking at the front door.

ABOUT THE AUTHOR

MAYA PRASAD is a South Asian American author, a Caltech graduate, and a former software engineer. She currently resides in the Pacific Northwest, where she enjoys hiking, kayaking, and writing stories with joyful representation for kids and teens. She is the author of the YA contemporary novel *Drizzle, Dreams, and Lovestruck Things*, and has had short fiction published in *Foreshadow: Stories to Celebrate the Magic of Reading and Writing YA*, *Cast of Wonders*, and *Voyage YA*. The Sejal Sinha STEM chapter book series was inspired by her own kiddo, who also has a favorite cheetah stuffie, an active imagination, and a trusty cardboard box. Visit her website MayaPrasad.com or find her on Instagram, Twitter, or TikTok @msmayaprasad.

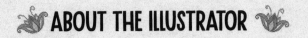

ABOUT THE ILLUSTRATOR

ABIRA DAS was born in India. As a child her biggest influences were watching her father drawing and painting, and her love of Disney animation movies. Throughout the year you will find her sipping tea, bookworming, listening to music, intensely doodling while having telephonic conversations, traveling the world, expanding her collection of soft toys and action figures, binge watching anything she can, and enhancing her world of Creativity.

READ & LEARN

with *simon* kids

Keep your child reading, learning, and having fun with Simon Kids!

A one-stop shop where you can **find downloadable resources, watch interactive author videos, browse books by reading level, and more!**

Visit us at
SimonandSchusterPublishing.com/ReadandLearn/

And follow us @SimonKids

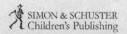

SIMON & SCHUSTER
Children's Publishing